SUPPLY AND DEMAND

by Marne Ventura

Cody Koala
An Imprint of Pop!
popbooksonline.com

abdopublishing.com
Published by Pop!, a division of ABDO, PO Box 398166, Minneapolis, Minnesota 55439.

Printed in the United States of America, North Mankato, Minnesota

032018
092018

THIS BOOK CONTAINS RECYCLED MATERIALS

Cover Photo: Africa Studio/Shutterstock Images
Interior Photos: Shutterstock Images, 1, 5 (top), 9, 13 (top), 19; iStockphoto, 5 (bottom left), 5 (bottom right), 6, 13 (bottom right), 13 (bottom left), 15, 20–21; Charlie Riedel/AP Images, 10; Red Line Editorial, 16, 17

Editor: Charly Haley
Series Designer: Laura Mitchell

Library of Congress Control Number: 2017963374

Publisher's Cataloging-in-Publication Data

Names: Ventura, Marne, author.
Title: Supply and demand / by Marne Ventura.
Description: Minneapolis, Minnesota : Pop!, 2019. | Series: Community economics |
Includes online resources and index.
Identifiers: ISBN 9781532160066 (lib.bdg.) | ISBN 9781532161186 (ebook) |
Subjects: LCSH: Supply and demand--Juvenile literature. | Community development--Juvenile literature.
| Regional economics--Juvenile literature. | Economic development--Juvenile literature. |
Community life--Juvenile literature.
Classification: DDC 330.9--dc23

Hello! My name is

Cody Koala

Pop open this book and you'll find QR codes like this one, loaded with information, so you can learn even more!

Scan this code* and others like it while you read, or visit the website below to make this book pop.

popbooksonline.com/supply-and-demand

*Scanning QR codes requires a web-enabled smart device with a QR code reader app and a camera.

Table of Contents

Chapter 1

Supply

Businesses sell things for money. The amount of things that a business has ready to sell is the **supply**.

Watch a video here!

A grocery store with only one apple left has a low supply. A store with a hundred apples has a greater supply.

Chapter 2

Demand

Demand is the amount of something that people want to buy. If just a few people want something, there is low demand.

Learn more here!

BEST BUY
DOOR BUSTERS
THURSDAY 5 PM
SONY
SAMSUNG
SHARP
NEW DOORBUSTERS REVEALED FRIDAY AND SATURDAY

When people want to buy a lot of something, there is high demand.

Sometimes people are willing to wait in long lines for an item that is in high demand.

Chapter 3

Price

Brett is a baker. He sells muffins. The **price** is $2.00 each.

Supply and demand are parts of the **economy.**

Learn more here!

Bella's new bakery sells muffins for \$2.00 each, too. Now there is a bigger supply of \$2.00 muffins.

But the demand for muffins is the same. Brett isn't selling as many muffins as he used to.

When a price is low, there is low supply because more people are buying that item. But if the price is too high, there is more supply because fewer people will buy that item.

Brett lowers the price of his muffins to $1.50. Now more people want to buy Brett's muffins because they are cheaper.

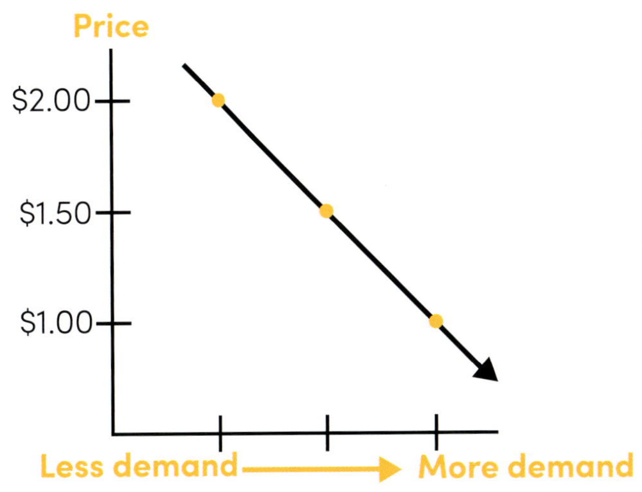

When a price is too high, there is low demand. When the price is low, there is high demand.

There is a higher demand for $1.50 muffins.

That is one way that supply and demand can help set prices.

Chapter 4

Seasonal Prices

Supply and demand may change because of a **season** or an event. In October, stores get a big supply of Halloween candy.

Complete an activity here!

Stores know a lot of people want candy for trick-or-treaters. The demand is high.

After Halloween, there is less demand for candy. To sell the candy they have left, stores lower the price.

Making Connections

Text-to-Self

Have you ever wanted to buy something that was in low supply?

Text-to-Text

What items have been in high demand for characters in your favorite books?

Text-to-World

How have you seen supply and demand in the real world?

Glossary

demand – the amount of something that people want to buy.

economy – the way all people act together to make, buy, and sell things.

price – how much money is needed to buy something.

season – a certain period of time each year.

supply – the amount of something that is ready to sell.

Index

Online Resources

popbooksonline.com

Thanks for reading this Cody Koala book!

Scan this code* and others like it in this book, or visit the website below to make this book pop!

popbooksonline.com/supply-and-demand

*Scanning QR codes requires a web-enabled smart device with a QR code reader app and a camera.